JUST BECAUSE

Mac Barnett

illustrated by

Isabelle Arsenault

WALKER BOOKS
AND SUBSIDIARIES

LONDON • BOSTON • SYDNEY • AUCKLAND

Why is the ocean blue?

They sing sad songs and cry blue tears.

What is the rain?

The tears
of flying fish.

Why do the leaves change colour?

By winter,
their branches have
all burned up.

Why do birds fly south for the winter?

To fetch
new leaves
for trees.

What happened to the dinosaurs?

Millions of years ago, thousands of asteroids fell on the earth.

But the dinosaurs
had planned for this.
They fastened themselves
to big balloons,
floated up to space,
and stayed there.

What are black holes?

The mouths of dinosaurs.

What is a volcano?

How do you tame a horse?

Wha a dese

What is the wind?

How big was a woolly mammoth?

What are freckles?

How were the pyramids built?

What is an echo?

What is quicksand?

What is
the moon?

What is
a rainbow?

Why do
we sneeze?

How tall
is the tallest
mountain?

How does
an egg become
a chicken?

What is
thunder?

What is
lightning?

Why do we have to sleep?

Because there
are some things we can
only see with our eyes
closed.